The

for inari

LOTHIAN
Children's Books

A Lothian Children's Book

Published in Australia and New Zealand
by Hachette Livre Australia Pty Limited
Level 17, 207 Kent Street, Sydney
NSW 2000
Website: www.hachettechildrens.com.au

Copyright © Shaun Tan 2001

First published 2001
Reprinted 2001, 2002, 2004, 2007
Paperback edition first published 2002
Reprinted 2003, 2004, 2005, 2006 (twice), 2007

National Library of Australia
Cataloguing-in-Publication data:

Tan, Shaun.
The red tree.

ISBN 978 0 7344 0172 4
ISBN 978 0 7344 0539 5 (paperback)

I. Title.

A823.3

Design by Shaun Tan
Colour reproduction by Scott Digital,
Port Melbourne
Printed in China by
Everbest Printing Co Ltd

sometimes the day begins
with nothing to look forward to

and things go from bad to worse

darkness

overcomes you

nobody understands

the world is a

deaf machine

without

sense

or

reason

sometimes you wait

and wait

and wait

and wait

and wait

and wait

and wait

but nothing ever happens

then all your **troubles** come at once

wonderful things

are

passing

you

by

terrible fates are
inevitable

sometimes
you just don't know
what you are
supposed
to
do

or

who

you

are

meant

to

be

or

where
you are

and the day seems to end
the way it began

but suddenly there it is
right in front of you

bright and vivid

quietly waiting

just as you imagined it would be